JPIC Goldf
Goldfinger, Jennifer P.
Hello, my name is Toby
Tiger

W9-AOK-682

$17.99
ocn932575687

First edition.

cat

dog

bird

For Eva and Esme—you're the best!
And a special thanks to Bobby and Cassidy.

ISBN 978-0-06-239951-9 (trade bdg.)

The artist used water color, gouache,
acrylic, colored pencil, chalk, crayons,
and digital collage to create the
illustrations for this book.

Typography by Chelsea C. Donaldson
16 17 18 19 20 SCP 10 9 8 7 6 5 4 3 2 1

First Edition

cat

dog

mouse

Toby liked being a cat
more than a boy.

He liked playing at home alone.

He was a frisky feline.

Until he learned he was going to school.

Then he was a timid kitten.

On the first day of school the teacher handed out name tags.

Toby fixed his, then said . . .

The other kids slid down the slides, swung on the swings,
and jumped over the jump ropes.

But Tiger scratched in the litter box,

pounced on a leaf,

and coughed up a hairball.

"Want to play?" asked Lottie.
Tiger hesitated,

then scampered away.

He climbed up a tree,

because that's what cats do.

Tiger purred.

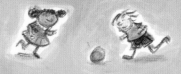

He looked down at the other kids having fun.

Maybe I'll join them after all, he thought.

But then he remembered . . .

cats can't climb
down trees!

But monkeys can.

"I'll show you how," said Pete.

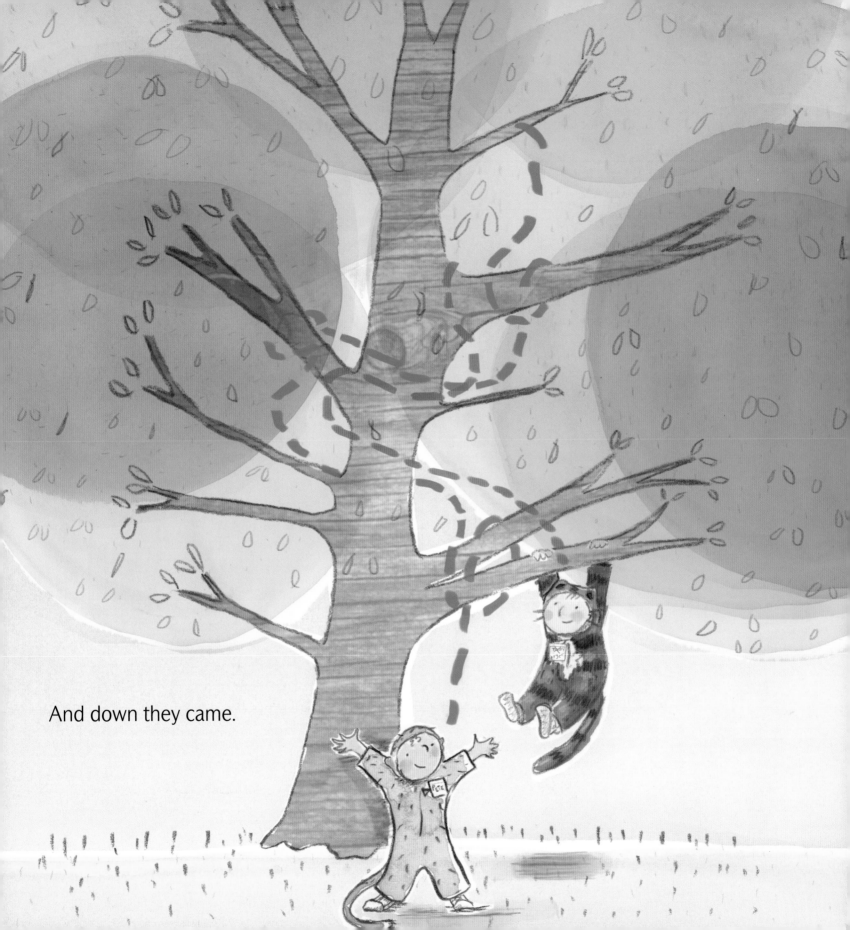

And down they came.

Tiger taught Pete how to swat like a cat.

Pete showed Tiger how to swing like a monkey.

At lunchtime, the hungry animals chased
each other inside for bananas and milk.

Tiger noticed Lottie. "Want to play with us?"

She hesitated . . .

then whistled,

"Tweet."

Tiger purred. Lottie chirped. Peter howled.

Sometimes Toby liked being a cat
more than a boy . . .

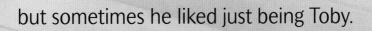
but sometimes he liked just being Toby.